The Child from Far Away

the Child from Far Away

E. T. A. HOFFMANN

RETOLD BY
DORIS ORGEL

ILLUSTRATED BY
MICHAEL EAGLE

ADDISON-WESLEY

 AN ADDISONIAN PRESS BOOK

Text copyright © 1971 by Doris Orgel
Illustrations copyright © 1971 by Michael Eagle

All rights reserved. Except for use in reviews,
no part of this book may be reproduced, utilized
or transmitted in any form or by any means,
electronic or mechanical, including photocopying,
recording or by any information storage and
retrieval system, without permission in writing
from the Publisher.
The Addison-Wesley Publishing Company, Inc.
Reading, Massachusetts 01867

Library of Congress catalog card number 74–110347
Printed in the United States of America
First printing
SBN: 201–02883–Z

TABLE OF CONTENTS

Sir Thaddeus von Brakel of Brakelheim

ONCE there was a nobleman, and his name was Sir Thaddeus von Brakel. He lived in the little village of Brakelheim. The four peasant families who also lived in this little village called him their *gracious lord*, even though he was poor and his everyday clothing was as coarse as theirs. He did have a fine green coat and a red vest with golden tassles—which, by the way, became him very well. But he only wore them on Sundays, when he drove with his wife and two children, Felix and Christlieb, to church in a larger village nearby.

Whenever anyone asked the peasants of Brakelheim how to find Sir Thaddeus, they always answered, "Go straight through the village, through the birch wood, up the hill, and there you'll find our gracious lord's castle."

Now, as everyone knows, a castle is a great, tall building with many windows and doors, many turrets and glittering weather vanes. But up on the hill where the birches stood, there was only a little, low house with a few small windows, and you couldn't even see it until you were right on top of it.

But have you ever stood before the tall portals of some great castle, shivering in a blast of cold air from inside, and quaking in your shoes because of the statues standing there like eerie watchmen, staring at you with dead eyes? And did you lose all desire to enter, and turn around and run?

Well, this could never have happened at Sir Thaddeus's door!

As you walked through the woods, the slender birches would have waved their leafy branches and welcomed you. And when you came nearer, you would have felt as though friendly voices from the small, mirror-bright windows and from the grape vines all along the walls were calling, "Tired wanderer, come in and rest!" Swallows flitting in and out of their nests under the eaves would have twittered their agreement. And an old stork would have looked down from the chimney and said, "I've lived here through many a summer, and I can find no better lodging on earth. Now if only I were cured of the traveler's itch, and if it didn't get so cold here in winter, and if firewood were not so dear, I'd never move from this place." For so pleasant and delightful, though certainly no castle, was the house of Sir Thaddeus von Brakel of Brakelheim.

Elegant Visitors

Lady von Brakel got up very early one morning and baked a splendid cake, with even more almonds and raisins in it than in an Easter cake. Meantime, Sir Thaddeus gave his green coat and red vest a thorough brushing. And Felix and Christlieb put on their best clothes.

"Children," said Sir Thaddeus, "Don't go running into the woods today. Stay quietly indoors, so you'll look neat and clean when your gracious Sir Uncle arrives."

By now the sun had come out bright and friendly from behind the mist, and sent its golden beams in through the windows. Out in the woods the morning wind whirred, and thrushes and finches pealed forth their gayest songs.

Christlieb sat silent and thoughtful at the table. She straightened the red ribbons on her dress. Then she tried to do her knitting, but it seemed to resist her fingers today.

Felix did not look at the picture book Sir Thaddeus had handed him. He gazed out at the beautiful birch wood where, on other mornings, he ran and played to his heart's content. "Oh, it's nice out there," he sighed.

Outside the window his big dog, Sultan, barked and growled. He started to run into the woods, then turned back and growled and barked some more, as if to call, "Felix, aren't you coming out? What are you doing cooped up in that stuffy room?"

"Oh, Mother dear, let me go," cried Felix. "Just for a little while, please!"

Lady von Brakel replied, "No, no, you stay here. If I let you, off you'd go, and Christlieb after you, whish, whish, through thorns and thickets and up. the trees! Then you'd come back all hot and dirty, and your uncle would say, "Who are those ugly little peasants?"

Felix snapped the picture book shut and said, "If our gracious Sir Uncle thinks peasant children are ugly, he can't have seen Vollard's Peter, or Hentschel's Anneliese, or any of us in this village, because there aren't any better-looking children anywhere in the world!"

"That's right," Christlieb agreed. "Isn't Schoolmaster's Gretel a pretty girl, even if she doesn't have any fancy red ribbons on her dress?"

"Nonsense," said their mother. "You don't understand what I'm trying to tell you."

So they had to sit and wait, and to make matters worse, smell the sweet cake, knowing that it wouldn't be cut until their uncle arrived. "If only he'd get here," they said, more and more impatiently.

Finally, loud clomping of horses was heard and a coach came rolling up. It was polished to a sheen and lavishly ornamented with gold. The coachman jumped down, opened the door and helped a tall, thin man step down.

The first thing Felix and Christlieb noticed about him was the big silver star on his chest. He went and laid his cheek twice against Sir Thaddeus's, and said, *"Bon jour*, my dear Cousin!"

Next the coachman helped a short, stout lady and two children—a boy and a girl—out of the coach, taking great care that they didn't stumble or fall.

When all the visitors were safely down, Felix and Christlieb did as their parents had told them: they kissed the uncle's hands, one each, and said, "A hearty welcome to you, dear, gracious Sir Uncle!" After that they kissed the aunt's hands, and said, "A hearty welcome to you too, dear, gracious Lady Aunt." Then they moved a step toward the children—but stopped, amazed. They had never seen such children before.

The boy had puffy pantaloons on, and a little scarlet jacket with lots and lots of gold thread and tassels on it. He had a shiny little saber by his side, and on his head was a peculiar red cap with a white feather sticking out. His face was pale and sallow, his eyes were dull and sleepy, and from the expression in them it was hard to tell if he was more shy than stupid or more stupid than shy.

The girl wore a white dress like Christlieb's, but with many more ribbons, and a lot of lace. Her hair was tightly braided, the braids were wound around her head, and on top of it all sat a shiny little crown. When Christlieb finally got herself to take the girl's hand, she snatched it away, and made such a mean, cry-baby face that Christlieb took fright and let her be.

Felix wanted to see the boy's saber a bit closer, so he reached for it.

"My saber, my saber! He's taking my saber away!" screamed the boy and ran and hid behind the tall, thin man.

Felix flushed and muttered, "I'm not taking your saber away, stupid!" Sir Thaddeus heard him. He started playing with the buttons on his vest—something he always did when he was embarrassed—and he whispered, "Now, Felix!"

"There, there, Adelgunde! There, there, Herrmann! These children are not going to hurt you," said the stout lady.

"They'd better not," said the tall thin man under his breath, and winked at the stout lady. Then he smiled in a rather sinister way, took Lady von Brakel by the hand, and led her into the house. Sir Thaddeus followed with the stout lady, Adelgunde and Herrmann clutching on to the train of her gown. Last came Christlieb and Felix. "Now, they'll cut the cake," Felix whispered in his sister's ear.

"Good!" she answered.

"After that we'll run into the woods," said Felix.

"And forget our stupid cousins," added Christlieb quietly.

Adelgunde and Herrmann were not allowed to have any cake. It wouldn't agree with them, their parents said. Instead they each got a dry cracker out of a box the coachman had brought along for them. But Felix and Christlieb ate their thick slices heartily, enjoying every bite.

The tall, thin man, Cyprianus von Brakel, was Sir Thaddeus von Brakel's cousin, but far more elegant. For he possessed the title of Count, which gave him the right to wear that great silver star on all his clothes, even on his nightshirt.

"Tell me, gracious Sir Uncle, did they make you a king?" asked Felix, for he had seen a picture in a picture book of a king with just such a star on his breast.

The uncle answered, "No, nephew, I'm not a king. But I am a most faithful servant and minister to one who is—." There was an eerie gleam in his eyes.

13

Felix shuddered. "Is what?" he asked.

"To one who is a mighty king," said the uncle mysteriously. Then he laughed as if it were all just a joke, turned to his wife and told her Felix had mistaken him for a king.

"Oh, sweet, rustic innocence!" exclaimed the lady. She then insisted that Sir Thaddeus bring the children out from a safe corner of the room, where they had settled themselves to eat their cake.

First their mother wiped the crumbs and raisins from their mouths. Then their gracious aunt kissed them, and pressed gaily wrapped packages into their hands. Their parents looked on with tears in their eyes at such kindness.

Felix opened his package, and found a bag of bonbons. With difficulty he bit into one, and Christlieb immediately did the same.

"No, dear children," cried the gracious uncle, "don't do that, you'll ruin your teeth! You must suck at the sugar coating until it melts in your mouths."

This piece of instruction made Felix angry, and he quite forgot his manners. "Uncle," he asked, "do you think I'm still a little baby? And must suck on things because I don't have teeth yet to bite with?" And with that he stuck another bonbon in his mouth and chewed it so hard that it crackled and crunched.

Sir Thaddeus had beads of sweat on his forehead, so embarrassed was he at Felix's behavior. And his mother whispered, "Felix, you're being very rude!"

That got Felix upset. He took what was left of the bonbon from his mouth, put it back in the bag and handed the bag to his uncle. "Please take back your bonbons, if I'm not supposed to eat them," he said.

Christlieb, who was used to following his example, did the same.

"Most honored, gracious Sir Cousin," Sir Thaddeus apologized, "please don't think too ill of them. You must understand, here in the country, in our meager circumstances— alas, who can bring up children as well behaved as yours?"

Count Cyprianus looked at Herrmann and Adelgunde, and gave an elegant, self-satisfied smile. Those two had long

since swallowed their crackers, and now sat silent and motionless on their chairs.

The stout lady smiled too, and said affectedly, "Yes, indeed, dear Sir Cousin, we are proud of how well brought up and how well taught our darling children are." And she gave Count Cyprianus a wink. Thereupon he shot a hundred questions at Herrmann and Adelgunde—about cities, rivers, mountains, strangely named and thousands of miles away.

Herrmann and Adelgunde answered them all with great speed. They proceeded to describe in minute detail the most frightful, most outlandish beasts from the farthest ends of the earth. They spoke of exotic trees and shrubs, and described the flavor of their fruits as if they had tasted them. Then Herrmann gave a precise account of some big battle three hundred years ago, and told all the names of the generals who'd been in it. Finally Adelgunde spoke of the stars, declaring that all sorts of strange figures and animals sat up there in the heavens.

This worried Felix. He moved closer to his mother and softly asked, "Mama, what's all that prattle about?"

"Hold your tongue, silly," said his mother, "that's not prattle, that's learning!"

"Astonishing, unheard of, to know so much at their tender age!" Sir Thaddeus exclaimed.

And his wife sighed, "oh dearie me, oh my, what angels they are! But what's to become of *our* little ones, here in the dreary countryside?"

"Yes, what's to become of them?" Sir Thaddeus joined in.

"Never you fear," said Count Cyprianus. "I shall attend to this matter immediately. I'll hire a tutor and send him to you. Yes, a very fine tutor who'll get some learning into these children's heads."

Sir Thaddeus and Lady von Brakel thanked him profusely.

Felix and Christlieb clung to each other. Something in their uncle's voice and manner sent a shiver down their backs.

The door opened, making them jump. But it was only the coachman, bringing in two large boxes. Herrmann and Adelgunde took them from him and handed them to Felix and Christlieb.

"Do you like toys, *mon cher*?" said Herrmann with a courtly bow. "Here, I've brought you some of the very best sort."

Felix hung his head. He felt bad, he didn't know why. He held the box awkwardly in his hands and muttered, "My name isn't Moncher, it's Felix."

Christlieb too, for some reason, felt closer to tears than smiling.

Soon afterwards the Count and his family prepared to leave. Sultan was barking in his usual friendly way, and jumping at the door. This brought Herrmann dashing back in, howling with terror.

"Don't worry, Sultan won't hurt you," said Felix. What are you howling about? He's not one of your frightful beasts, he's just an ordinary dog! And even if he did attack you, which he won't, you've got your saber, haven't you?"

That didn't help. Herrmann howled on, till the coachman picked him up and carried him into the coach. And suddenly Adelgunde, infected by her brother, or Heaven knows why else, started howling loudly too, and that upset Christlieb so *she* started sobbing and weeping. In the midst of all this uproar, Count Cyprianus von Brakel's coach rolled away, and so ended the elegant visit.

As soon as the coach was out of sight, Sir Thaddeus threw off his green coat and red vest, put his coarse jacket on, took a deep breath, stretched and said, "Thank God!"

The children, too, tore off their Sunday clothes, and felt free and gay. "Into the woods!" Felix shouted, and tried to see how high he could jump for sheer joy.

"First, don't you want to see what Herrmann and Adelgunde brought you?" asked their mother. And Christlieb, who'd been eyeing the boxes curiously, agreed they should. There'd be time to run into the woods afterwards.

But Felix said, "What could be so great about anything that clown in pantaloons and his sister with the ribbons brought us? Oh, he's very learned, he can prattle fast enough about lions and bears, he says he can hunt elephants, and next thing you know, he's scared of my Sultan! He has a saber by his side, but howls and screams and crawls under the table— he's some huntsman, that Cousin Pantaloons!"

But Christlieb insisted, "Please, dear, good Felix, let's just open the boxes a tiny little bit!"

So to please her, Felix put off running into the woods and sat down patiently with her at the table on which the boxes stood.

Their mother opened them. And now, dear reader, remember Christmases and birthdays! Think how you shouted with delight at the sight of shiny tin soldiers, tiny organ grinders, dolls in beautiful dresses, doll furniture, and wonderful bright picture books lying all around! Such joy as you had

19

then, Felix and Christlieb had now. For the boxes were full of a rich assortment of the darlingest, shiniest things, as well as of tasty treats to eat. The children clapped their hands and cried, "How beautiful, how beautiful!"

Everything was to their liking, except for another bag of bonbons. "No, don't!" said Christlieb as Felix was about to throw it out the window. So instead he threw some bonbons to Sultan who meanwhile had come back inside. Sultan sniffed at them and turned away. "You see," said Felix, triumphantly, "not even Sultan wants to eat those nasty things."

Of all the toys, the one that pleased Felix most was a stately little huntsman. He had a thread hanging down from under his coat. When you pulled the thread, he took aim and shot at a target fixed three spans in front of him. Next best, Felix liked a little harpist who, when you turned a little screw, made a bow and played, *quinkalink,* on his harp. Then, too, he liked a rifle and a hunting knife, both made of wood and silvered over, and a handsome hunting bag.

What Christlieb loved most was a beautiful doll with a large wardrobe of dainty clothes.

By the time they had looked at everything, both children had forgotten about the woods for that day. They played with their toys until late in the evening. Then they went to bed.

What Happened to the New Toys in the Woods

Next morning the children went straight to the boxes, took their toys out and played and played. Meanwhile the sun shone bright and friendly through the window, the birches whispered in the whirring wind, and finches and thrushes sang their merriest, loveliest songs.

Suddenly Felix had a tight, woeful feeling around his heart. He put down the little toy huntsman, gun and hunting bag. "Come, Christlieb," he cried. "It's nicer outside, let's run into the woods!"

Christlieb had just finished undressing her doll and was about to dress her again. She didn't want to go. "Please, Felix," she said, "Let's play just a little longer."

"I know what!" said Felix. "Let's take our toys with us! I'll stick the hunting knife in my belt, and I'll sling the gun over my shoulder so I'll look like a real hunter. The little huntsman and harpist can come too. And you can bring your doll. Come on, let's go!"

Quickly Christlieb dressed the doll. Then the children ran into the woods with their toys. They found a nice green spot, and settled down and played.

"You know what, Felix?" said Christlieb after a while, "your little harpist isn't such a very good musician. Listen: Doesn't that *ting-ting, ping-ping* of his sound ugly out here? The birds don't like it either. Look how they're peeping at him from the bushes! They wish he'd stop spoiling their songs!"

Felix turned the harpist's screw a bit harder to see if he could play any better. "You're right" he agreed, "he does sound awful! I'm ashamed of him! What must the little finch be thinking, that's looking at me so reproachfully? Come on, harpist, you can do better!" And Felix turned the screw so hard that—*crack, crack!*—the box on which the little harpist stood broke into a thousand pieces. The harpist's arms broke off and fell crumbling to the ground.

"Oh! Oh!" cried both children, dismayed.

"Oh well," said Felix after a moment, "he was a bad musician. Besides, he bowed and scraped just like my Cousin Pantaloons!" And he threw the harpist away, far into the thickest bushes. "I like the huntsman a lot better, he hits the target every time!"

Felix made the huntsman take aim at the target fixed in front of him, and shoot, over and over and over. After a while he got bored and said, "What good is a target that never moves? A huntsman's business is to shoot at stags and hares that go running wild through the woods!" With that he broke the target off. "Now, little huntsman," shoot freely!" he cried. And he pulled and pulled on the thread—but no matter how hard he pulled, the huntsman's arms hung limp by his sides.

"Ha, ha!" Felix laughed, "You can't! And are you scared of dogs, too? If a dog came along now, would you take your gun and run, just like Cousin Pantaloons did with his saber by his side? Oh, you're a stupid, no-good fellow!" Felix hurled him after the harpist into the thicket. "Come on, Christlieb," he shouted, "let's run!"

"Yes, let's," said Christlieb, "and my doll can run with us, that'll be fun."

So they took the doll by one arm each, and started running, fast, fast, through shrubs and thickets, down hills and

23

away, until they came to a pond where tall bullrushes grew, where Sir Thaddeus sometimes came to shoot wild ducks.

Here they stopped. "Let's wait a while," said Felix. "I've got my gun, who knows, maybe I'll shoot a duck in the rushes, the way Father does."

At that moment Christlieb looked down and cried, "Look what happened to my doll!"

The poor thing looked a wreck. While they were running, the underbrush had ripped her clothes; also she had broken both her little legs; and her once-pretty wax face was all scratched and ugly now. "Oh my doll, my beautiful doll!" Christlieb wailed.

"Well, now you know what sort of presents our cousins brought us," said Felix. "That doll's a clumsy clod, she couldn't even run with us without getting herself all torn and ripped up. Come on, let me have her!"

Christlieb handed him the doll. Without further ado, Felix threw her in the pond.

Christlieb couldn't keep from crying.

"Don't be sad," Felix comforted her. "I'll tell you what: if I shoot a duck, I'll let you have its best wing feathers!" Just then came a rustling in the reeds. Felix aimed his rifle—but then he looked at it hard and said, "How stupid of me! Don't I need powder and lead? And even if I had some, could I load it into a wooden rifle? Oh well, I've still got my hunting knife —but that's wooden, too! It can't cut a thing! Of course that explains it, my cousin's saber was wooden as well—that's why he couldn't use it when he was so scared of Sultan. Oh, I see it all now: Cousin Pantaloons tried to make me into as big a fool as he is, with those toys that pretend they're some- thing wonderful, but are really absolutely useless!" And he hurled the rifle, hunting knife and hunting bag far out into the pond. Then he and Christlieb went home.

"Children, where are your toys?" asked their mother.

So Felix told her how badly deceived they had been in his huntsman, harpist, gun, hunting knife, hunting bag and Christlieb's doll.

"Oh, you ignorant children!" cried Lady von Brakel. "Too ignorant to know what to do with such beautiful toys!"

But Sir Thaddeus said, "Let the children be, maybe they were right, who knows?"

And neither the children, nor Lady von Brakel, nor he himself knew exactly what he meant. . . .

The Child From Far Away

One morning very early, Felix and Christlieb ran into the woods.

"Don't be long," their mother called. She wanted them to be indoors as much as possible these days to practice their reading and writing, so that when the tutor arrived he should think well of them.

"Let's run and jump as hard as we can!" called Felix to his sister.

So they played chasing games but soon got tired of all the ones they tried. And oddly enough, all sorts of things happened today to annoy them: the wind blew Felix's cap off. The cap caught in the bushes. Felix tripped. And just when he was running his fastest, he fell, smack, on his nose. Christlieb's dress caught on a thorn bush. She stubbed her toe on a pointed stone, and it hurt so much, she cried.

"Maybe we'd better go home," said Felix. But instead he threw himself down in the shade of a tree. Christlieb did too, and there they sat, disgruntled, staring at the ground. "Oh, if we only still had our toys!" sighed Christlieb.

"They still wouldn't be any good," grumbled Felix. "We'd just break them and throw them away all over again. Listen, Christlieb, maybe Mother was right, those toys were too good for us because we're so ignorant and all."

"Yes," said Christlieb, "if we were clever like our cousins, we'd still have our toys." And they both started to cry, "Oh, we're poor, ignorant children and have nothing to play with, nothing!"

Suddenly they stopped. "Christlieb, do you see—?" "Felix, do you hear—?" they asked, gazing at the bushes opposite.

Out of the deep shadows of those bushes gleamed a brightness. It hovered like a moonbeam over the leaves. The leaves began to tremble. And through the murmur of the woods came a soft, sweet sound, like the wind gliding over a harp and caressing its slumbering chords awake.

The children felt very strange. All their sadness left them, yet tears stood in their eyes. The sweet sound grew louder, the brightness gleamed brighter still, their hearts beat faster— and in the center of the brilliance they saw the face of a child. "Come to us," they called, reaching out with their arms, "oh, come to us!"

"I'm coming," called a voice, and gently, as if carried by the breeze, the child came floating over to them.

How the Child From Far Away Played with Felix and Christlieb

"I heard you crying, what's wrong?" asked the child.

"We didn't really know," said Felix. "But now it feels as if all that was wrong was, you weren't with us."

"That's right," said Christlieb, "and now you're here, and we're happy again. Why did you stay away so long?"

For they both felt as if they had long known and played with the child, and as if their dear playmate had only lately not been coming to them.

"You see," Felix started to explain, "we had nothing to play with, because I threw away the toys my Cousin Panta-loons gave me, and—."

"Felix, Felix," laughed the child, "those toys weren't for you! You have lots to play with, just look at the wonderful things all around!"

"Where? Where?" asked Felix and Christlieb.

"Look around," said the child.

They did. And now they saw bright-eyed flowers peeking up from the thick grass and woolly moss; they saw pebbles of all colors, and tiny golden bugs dancing up and down, buzzing songs.

"Let's build a palace," said the child, bending down for some pebbles. Felix and Christlieb picked up pebbles too. The child put one on top of the other—and soon columns arose, glistening in the sunlight, and an airy, golden roof arched over them.

The child bent down and touched the flowers. No sooner done than the flowers reached up and clasped one another, forming fragrant archways for Felix and Christlieb to go skipping through.

The child clapped its hands—and the palace roof buzzed asunder, for it was a thousand tiny golden bugs that had been stretching out their wings, and now they flew away. And the columns crumbled gently down into the woodland stream, and the flowers bent their heads and gazed into its ripples, listening to the murmur it made.

Now the child picked blades of grass, broke little twigs off bushes, scattered them before Felix and Christlieb—and out of the grass blades grew the most beautiful dolls imaginable, and out of the twigs grew tiny, dainty huntsmen. The dolls danced around Christlieb. They let her take them in her lap and whispered to her tenderly, "Christlieb, be good to us!" The huntsmen blew their horns and cried, "Halloo,

halloo, let's go a-hunting!" Then little hares came leaping from the bushes, and dogs behind them, and the huntsmen's guns went *bang, bang, bang*—oh, it was wonderful! Then, slowly, it all faded away.

"Where are the dolls, where are the huntsmen?" called Christlieb and Felix.

"They're all at your command," said the child. "They can be with you whenever you want. But wouldn't you rather run through the woods with me for a while?"

"Yes!" they answered.

So the child took them by the hands, and off they went— but you couldn't call it running. Up in the air they rose, float- ing over woods and fields, with birds flying and singing about them.

"Good morning, children, good morning, friend Felix!" called the stork when they passed him.

"I promise I won't eat up any little pigeons," screeched the hawk, "just don't hurt me," and swung away.

Felix shouted with joy. But Christlieb started to be afraid, and called, "I'm getting out of breath, oh dear, I'm going to fall!"

So then they alighted in a clearing. "Now I'll play you a woodland tune," said the child, took a little golden horn, and played on it. Birds came and perched on twigs close by and sang along, and all the woods resounded.

Then, slowly, the tones faded, and finally only the softest whisper was heard from the bushes into whose shadows the child had disappeared, calling, "I'll come again tomorrow!"

Felix and Christlieb felt more joyful than ever before in their lives, and ran home to tell their parents all they had seen and done.

What Their Parents Said and What Then Befell

"Could it have been a dream?" wondered Sir Thaddeus von Brakel. "But how could they both have dreamed the same dream at the very same time?"

"Don't think so hard about it, dear husband," said his wife. "I have a hunch that child is none other than Schoolmaster's Gottlieb from the big village. Probably he came running over and put those wild ideas into the children's heads. Well, he won't do it again, I'll see to that."

Sir Thaddeus thought differently. He called Felix and Christlieb, and asked them to tell him what the child had looked like.

They said the child was more beautiful than words could tell—but that was all they could agree on.

"She had a filmy soft dress made of rose petals," said Christlieb.

"No," said Felix, "his clothes were green, like leaves in the sun. But he isn't any schoolmaster's boy!" Felix had to laugh at that. "He knows too much about hunting, he must come from wherever love of the woods comes from! And one day he'll be the world's best huntsman!"

"Oh Felix, how can that little girl grow up to be a huntsman? She may know about hunting, but she knows lots more about dolls," said Christlieb. She was sure the child was a girl. Felix was sure the child was a boy. And neither would give in to the other. Lady von Brakel shook her head. It was all stuff and nonsense, she said.

But Sir Thaddeus thought, "Maybe I'll follow the children into the woods and see what child it is that plays with them . . . No, if I did that, I might spoil something wonderful . . . No, no, I'd better not . . ."

Next morning, when Felix and Christlieb ran into the woods, the child was waiting for them, and made up more wonderful games.

When they had played a while, the child called, "Alder bushes, tell us, what did Friend Morning Wind bring?"

The alder bushes shook their twigs and laughed and whispered so clearly that Felix and Christlieb understood every word, "Pretty things, pretty things! Kisses from the queen who lives behind the blue mountains, and sweet perfumes—."

"He wheedled those perfumes from *us*!" interrupted the flowers jealously. "Children, don't listen to those alder bushes. Listen to us, look at us, we love you so!"

Christlieb kneeled down and touched them. "We love you too," she said.

"Yes," said Felix, "but we also love the green woods that shelter and protect us."

"Well spoken, lad," came a rustling from the tall black hemlocks, "and don't you be afraid when Friend Stormwind comes, and he and we quarrel a bit!"

"Quarrel and crackle and creak all you want, you great giants," Felix shouted back, "that's music to any brave huntsman's ears!"

"Why always speak of hunting," gurgled the forest stream, "of stormwinds and of quarreling? I come from far-off lands, from deep down in the earth, I'll tell you tales, and always new ones, wave on wave, and ever on. I'll show you pictures, just look into my mirror face, and see the sky, the trees, bushes, flowers and your own dear selves!"

They looked at the stream and listened to its tales till the sun began to sink behind the mountains and the child said, "Now the nightingale's calling me home."

"Let's fly a little first," begged Felix.

"But not too high, or I'll get dizzy," said Christlieb.

So the child took them by the hands, and they floated up into the gold and purple dusk, birds crowding and noising about them. Far away, in the blazing clouds, Felix saw castles of ruby, amber and gold. "Christlieb, look at the castles!" he shouted.

Christlieb stopped looking down at the ground, and forgot to be afraid. She looked into the distance, and she saw the castles, too.

"Let's fly on, we'll soon be there!" called Felix.

But the child said, "No, we won't get there today . . ."

Felix and Christlieb felt as if in a dream—and had no idea how in the world they got home again, safely to their father and mother.

About the Child's Distant Home

In the loveliest spot in the woods, by the whispering bushes, beside the stream, the child had built a canopy of lilies and tulips. Under this canopy they now sat, all three.

"Friend, where do you come from?" Felix asked. "Where do you always disappear to so fast?"

"Do you know, little girl" said Christlieb, "our mother thinks you're Schoolmaster's Gottlieb!" and she laughed.

"Hush, silly," said Felix to his sister. And asked again, "Where do you live? Tell us, so we can find your house in the winter when it's too cold to play in the woods."

The child looked almost sad and said, "Isn't it enough that I come and play with you every day? Why ask about my home? If I said it's beyond the blue mountains, and if you ran for days and always on, till you stood on those mountain tops, you'd see still more mountains, just as far away, and when you'd have reached those mountains, you'd see still more, and so it would go on and on—you'd never reach my home.''

"Oh," cried Christlieb mournfully, "then you must live hundreds of miles away, and can only come on short visits!"

"But Christlieb, dear," said the child, "whenever you long for me in your heart, I can be with you at once, with games and wonders from my home—isn't that enough?"

"No," said Felix. "Your home must be the most wonderful place in the world. I want to go there, no matter how far or how hard it is to get there."

"It *is* the most wonderful place in the world," said the child. "And my mother is queen there and reigns in glitter and glory."

36

"Then you're a prince!" said Felix. "A princess!" said Christlieb. And both were struck with awe.

"That's true," said the child.

"And you live in a beautiful palace," said Felix.

"Yes," said the child, "in an even more beautiful palace than the ones you saw in the clouds. It has tall, tall crystal columns, and the blue sky above them for a roof. Under that roof the clouds sail by, dawn comes, dusk comes, and the bright stars dance their rounds. Oh my dear playmates, you've heard tell of fairies, maybe you've guessed it: My mother is their queen. And how she loves children! She used to arrange lovely parties for them . . . Listen: My mother's spirits would hang a rainbow from one end of the palace to the other, and build her a diamond throne underneath, so it caught and reflected all the colors. Mother would sit there, and they'd touch their harps and clang their cymbals, and then

singers would sing with voices to make your hearts melt with delight. Those singers are birds, bigger than eagles, with feathers of a purple such as you've never seen. And everything in the palace and gardens would come alive with children playing—chasing through the bushes, throwing themselves among the flowers, climbing trees, letting the wind rock them to and fro, picking fruits sweeter than any on earth, playing with deer and other tame animals, running up and down the rainbow, and some even climbing on the golden pheasants' backs and flying through the clouds."

"Oh, wonderful!" cried Felix and Christlieb, "Oh take us to your home!"

But the child said, "I can't. It's too far away . . ."

Felix and Christlieb grew sad and looked silently down at the ground.

About the Evil Minister at the Fairy Queen's Court

"Listen, I must tell you—," said the child in a troubled way, "from now on I can only come to you secretly. My mother has an enemy whom she banished from her court, and while he roams about I'm not safe anywhere."

"I'd like to see that enemy!" cried Felix, jumping up and brandishing a stick. "I'll fight him! So will my father! We'll catch him and lock him up in a tower!"

"Alas," said the child, "sticks cannot hurt him, and towers cannot hold him."

"Then he must be a terrible monster if you're afraid of him," said Christlieb. "Tell us who he is."

The child began to explain, "Queens have ministers just as kings do—."

"Yes," Felix interrupted, "our uncle the Count is a minister, he wears a star on his breast. Do your mother's ministers wear stars too?"

"No," said the child, "because some of them *are* stars, and others don't wear any coats to pin them to. You see, my mother's ministers are spirits. Some float in the air, others live in flames, still others live in water, and wherever they are, they carry out my mother's wishes.

"But an evil spirit found his way to her. He called himself Pepasilio. He was very learned, he said, and knew more and could do more than all Mother's other spirits put together. So Mother took him on as a minister—and soon he showed what he was really like.

"He tried to spoil whatever the other ministers did, especially the children's parties. He grabbed children down from trees, stopped them from running and jumping, made them creep around on all fours with their heads down. He put poison into the purple birds' beaks, he hated their singing. Worst of all, he had a nasty black fluid which he and his helpers spread all over the palace, all over the flowers, even over the rainbow, so everything looked sad and dead, and nothing gleamed or glittered anymore. When he was done, he laughed a horrible laugh and screamed, 'Now everything is as it should be! Queen, you have no more majesty, I have it all now, it's mine!' Right before our eyes he changed himself into a fly with a monstrous long thin nose. Hideously buzzing, he mounted her throne. So now she knew—we all knew—who the deceitful 'Pepasilio' really was: none other than the fiendish Pepser, king of the gnomes.

"But he had underestimated my mother's forces. Quickly her ministers of air drew around her and fanned sweet breezes to her; the ministers of fire rushed about in waves of flame, while the singers, with freshly cleaned beaks, sang out resounding songs. In this way they kept my mother from having to see ugly Pepser, or hear his buzzing, or feel his foul breath. Then suddenly the Pheasant Baron snatched him up, all but crushing him with his beak, flew high, high up into the air, and hurled him down to earth.

"That instant, Pepser's black fluid flowed away of its own accord. Children came with fly swatters and swatted his helpers, and soon everything was blooming and shiny and glittery as before.

"When Pepser reached earth, he lay screaming and couldn't move. Finally his cousin, a great blue toad, came creeping by. She carried him home, and nursed his bruises and wounds. And now, you see, he's trying to get revenge on my mother by chasing me, and I never know in what shape or form, or where or when he might suddenly pounce . . ."

Christlieb cried bitterly to think the child was in such danger. But Felix said, "If that Pepser's nothing but a great big fly, I'll chase him with my father's fly swatter, I'll swat him so hard on his nose, his cousin toad will never get him home!"

How the Tutor Came and the Children Were Afraid

The children ran home, bursting to tell about all the child had told them. But they stopped in the doorway, as if frozen into statues, for a strange, amazing person came striding toward them, muttering under his breath.

"This is your tutor," said Sir Thaddeus, "whom your gracious uncle has sent. Hurry up, children, greet him politely."

But the children could only stare, so weird-looking was their tutor. He was short, only a few inches taller than Felix, and very heavy set, except for his legs which were extremely thin and stuck out oddly from the rest of him. His head was almost square, and his face extraordinarily ugly, with a far too long, pointed nose, thick brownish-red cheeks, a broad mouth and small, beady protruding eyes that seemed to pierce Felix and Christlieb with their gaze. He wore a jet-black wig, was dressed in black from head to toe, and his name was Master Ink.

"What's the matter with you?" said Lady von Brakel to the children. "Master Ink must think you very rude. Go on, give him your hands, nicely now!"

They made themselves do it. But when Master Ink took their hands they jumped back with wails of pain.

Master Ink burst out laughing and showed them a needle he had been hiding, with which he had stuck them.

Christlieb cried. Felix muttered, but not loud enough for Master Ink to hear, "Don't try that again, little fat-belly!"

"Why, Master Ink," exclaimed Sir Thaddeus, "how could you do such a thing?"

"That's just my way," he answered, "somehow I can't manage *not* to." And he gave a laugh that creaked like a broken rattle.

"You're a humorous man, Master Ink," said Sir Thaddeus, but did not sound amused.

"Well now, let me see how it stands with these wretches' education," said Master Ink. "Hmmm, hmm." And he started to question the children just as their uncle had questioned Herrmann and Adelgunde.

But unlike their cousins, Felix and Christlieb could not reel off the answers.

"I see, I see!" said Master Ink. "No education at all!"

He did not take into account that Felix and Christlieb could write very neatly, and read very well, and knew many fine tales from books they had read. That was all nothing, said the tutor. He would fill their heads full of *important* things, even if it took twenty-four hours a day for years!

Oh dear, now they were never allowed to run in the woods! They had to sit inside and parrot whatever Master Ink said, even when they couldn't make head or tail of it. Oh, how heavy their hearts were, and with what longing they looked out the window!

Often they thought they heard, amidst bird songs and trees' whisperings, the child's sweet voice calling, "Felix, Christlieb! Where are you? Aren't you coming to play with me? I'll show you some pretty pebbles, I'll build you a flower palace, we'll swing ourselves into the clouds and build castles in the air! Come, oh please, come!"

That pulled them, all but bodily, into the woods, and they couldn't look at Master Ink any more or listen to what he was saying. So then, *crash*, went his fists on the table, he hummed and mumbled, and made strange, angry noises, "*Pmmm—sim—srr*—stop that staring out the window and pay attention, instantly!"

But Felix had had enough. "Let me be, Master Ink, go look for Cousin Pantaloons, ask *him* those questions! I'm going into the woods! Come, Christlieb, the child's out there, waiting for us!"

Off they ran. But just outside the door Master Ink nabbed them. Felix fought and fought, but could not get free. Then faithful Sultan came to his aid. Sultan had taken a strong dislike to Master Ink. Whenever the tutor was near he growled, thrashed with his tail at those thin little legs, sometimes almost knocking him over. Now Sultan leaped, and brought his front paws roughly down on the tutor's collar. The tutor broke into pitiful screams and had to let go of Felix.

The screams brought Sir Thaddeus running. "Down!" he commanded, and Sultan released Master Ink.

"What's happening here?" asked Sir Thaddeus.

Master Ink replied, "Those wretches tried to run away!"

"He never lets us go out in the woods," said Felix and Christlieb.

Sir Thaddeus scolded the children. But he felt sorry for them and urged Master Ink to take them out for daily walks.

Master Ink objected. "If you had a civilized garden with box hedges and a picket fence, I could walk there with the children at noon. But why go into the wild woods?"

The children didn't want him to. They couldn't bear the thought of Master Ink setting foot there.

How the Children and Master Ink Went Walking in the Woods, and What Happened Then

Nevertheless, he did.

"You don't like it out here, do you, Master Ink?" said Felix as they passed the whispering bushes.

Master Ink made a sour face. "There aren't even any proper paths," he complained. "One tears one's stockings! And one can't speak a sensible word with all those silly birds screeching their heads off."

"I can tell you don't know anything about singing," said Felix. "You can't hear the morning wind talking to the bushes or the stream telling its stories."

"And you don't like flowers, either," said Christlieb, "do you, Master Ink?"

Master Ink's face turned a darker shade of reddish-brown. He flailed with his hands and shouted, "Who put that foolishness in your heads? That's all we'd need, the wind, bushes and stream mixing into intelligent conversation! Birdsong, too, I can do without. Flowers I like well enough, if they're neatly stuck into vases. Anyway, flowers grow in gardens, not out here."

"But Master Ink," said Christlieb, "can't you see those lilies-of-the-valley? They're looking at you with bright, friendly eyes!"

"What? Flowers with eyes? Ha, ha, pretty eyes!" Master Ink reached down, tore a whole bunch of lilies-of-the-valley up by the roots and threw them in the thicket. The children felt as if they heard a moaning sound go through the woods. Christlieb cried. Felix gritted his teeth.

Just then a little finch flew by, right past Master Ink's nose, onto a twig, and started a song.

"I do believe that is a mockingbird making fun of me," said Master Ink. He picked up a stone, threw it, and the poor finch fell down dead.

Now Felix couldn't contain himself. "Horrible Master Ink," he shouted, "what did that poor bird do to you? Oh child from far away, where are you? Come to us, fly with us, I won't stay here with this horrible tutor, I want to fly to your home!"

And Christlieb sobbed, "Come save us, or Master Ink will kill us just like he did the flowers and the bird!"

"What's this about a child from far away?" asked the tutor.

Just then there was a louder whispering in the bushes, mixed in with heart–rending tones as of muted, distant bells. In clouds drifting down, first the face, then the form of the child appeared. It wrung its hands, tears flowed from its eyes. "Farewell, my playmates," it called, "I can't come to you anymore. The Gnome-King Pepser has you in his power. Oh my poor playmates, good-bye!" With that the child disappeared into the air.

Then, buzzing and humming hideously, Master Ink changed himself into a fly right in front of Felix and Christlieb's eyes. But, horrendous to behold, he kept his human face and some of his clothing. With more buzz and humming, he flew up into the air—to catch the child, Christlieb and Felix were sure. Shaking with terror, they ran, ran, ran away. They dared not look up till they reached a clearing. Then they saw, high in the clouds, a dot descending. It was bright as a star. "It's the child!" cried Christlieb.

The star-like thing grew larger, tones like trumpet blasts could be heard, and soon the children saw that the star-like thing was not the child, but a beautiful bird with golden feathers. With mighty wing beats and loud singing it alighted in the woods.

"Ha!" shouted Felix, "that must be the Pheasant Baron! He'll bite Master Ink to death, the child is safe, and so are we! Come, Christlieb, quick, let's run home and tell Father and Mother what happened."

How Sir Thaddeus Chased Master Ink Away

Father and Mother sat outside their little house and watched the sun start to sink behind the blue mountains. On a table before them was their supper, a pitcher of milk and a plate of bread and butter.

"I wonder where Master Ink can be so long with the children," said Sir Thaddeus. "First he didn't want to go out into the woods at all, now he won't come back. Altogether an amazing man, that tutor. I almost wish he'd never come. I didn't like him sticking the children with that needle.... And I'm not so impressed with his learning. He may know exactly what sort of spats the Grand Mogul of Malpimpanolia wears, but he can't tell a lime tree from a chestnut tree! I don't see how the children can respect him."

"I feel the same, dear husband," said Lady von Brakel. "I was so pleased when your cousin the Count promised us a master for them, but why did it have to be Master Ink? I don't know about his learning, all I know is, he revolts me, especially his greed! Wherever there's a pitcher of milk or beer, he comes buzzing around it, and if I leave the sugar jar open, he sniffs and picks at it till I put the lid down, smack, on his nose, then off he goes, mumbling and mad—but look!"

Felix and Christlieb came running through the birches. "Hurray, hurray!" Felix shouted. "The Pheasant Baron bit Master Ink to death!" And Christlieb shouted, all out of breath, "Mama, that Master Ink's no tutor, he's the Gnome-

King Pepser, and he's a horrible big fly with a wig and shoes and stockings on!" All excitedly they told how the Gnome-King was the Fairy Queen's enemy, and that he would surely have caught the child from far away if it hadn't been for the Pheasant Baron.

Their parents looked bewildered. "Are you sure you haven't been dreaming?" asked Sir Thaddeus.

Everything had happened just as they said, the children insisted, and Master Ink, or rather, Pepser, was doubtless lying dead somewhere in the woods.

"Oh, children, children," cried Lady von Brakel, "what wild imaginings! Whatever will become of you?"

But Sir Thaddeus mused about what they had told, and said, "Children, I admit it, I myself thought Master Ink peculiar right from the beginning. Neither your mother nor I are pleased with him. But tell me, supposing such ugly things as gnomes really do exist in the world, how can anybody be both a tutor and a fly?"

"I wouldn't have believed it myself," said Felix, "if the child hadn't told me, and if I hadn't seen Master Ink turn into a fly with my own two eyes. He really is Pepser! He only pretends to be Master Ink!"

"Hush," said Sir Thaddeus, "however that may be, one thing's sure, the Pheasant Baron didn't bite him dead—because here he comes now, out of the woods!"

The children fled screaming into the house—for indeed, Master Ink, eyes ablaze, wig all rumpled, approached with horrible humming. He staggered crazily from side to side, and bumped his head against trees so one could hear them cracking.

When he arrived, he instantly snatched the pitcher, making the milk run over, and drank it with disgusting noises.

"In Heaven's name, Master Ink, what are you doing?" Lady von Brakel exclaimed.

"Have you gone mad, is the Evil One after you?" shouted Sir Thaddeus.

Loudly buzzing, Master Ink, swung himself up on the table, tucked his coat tails under him, and seated himself on the plate of bread and butter. Then, buzzing still louder, down again, over to the door—but he couldn't get in because the children had locked the door. So he tried all the windows, *rap, rap,* making the glass clink and clank. Sir Thaddeus tried to catch him, but Master Ink kept escaping his grasp. Then Felix burst out of the house, holding the big fly swatter. "Take it, Father," he shouted. "Swat ugly Pepser dead!"

Sir Thaddeus took it, and now the chase began in earnest.

52

Felix, Christlieb and Lady von Brakel whisked the napkins and cloth off the table and swung them about in the air, driving Master Ink this way and that, while Sir Thaddeus kept swatting, but missing every time. The chase grew ever wilder. *Zumm, zumm, zimm, zimm, brrrm, trrr*, went the master, up and down and all around; *clip, clap* fell Sir Thaddeus's blows, thick as hail; and with *huss, huss, huss*, Felix, Christlieb and Lady von Brakel kept driving the enemy on. Finally Sir Thaddeus struck him a blow, *swat*, right on his coat tails, pinning him to the ground.

But just as Sir Thaddeus was about to swat him again, he swung himself high once more, and with redoubled strength and *buzz* and *hmmm* went storming away toward the birches.

Sir Thaddeus and Lady von Brakel breathed a sigh of relief.

54 The children jumped up and down again for joy and shouted, "Hurrah!" at the top of their voices.

What Further Happened in the Woods
After Master Ink Was Chased Away

Felix and Christlieb thought now that Pepser had fled, the child would surely come back and play with them as before. And they hurried out into the woods.

But everything was strangely still. No finches or thrushes, no birds at all did they hear. The bushes did not whisper. The stream did not burble. Only faint, frightened sighs whispered through the air. Black clouds welled up, the stormwind began to howl, the hemlocks to crackle and creak, and in the distance thunder rumbled.

Christlieb trembled and clung to Felix. He said, "What are you so frightened of? A storm's brewing, that's all, and we'll have to hurry home."

They started running, but—they didn't know how it happened—instead of coming out of the woods, they came deeper and deeper in. Heavy raindrops fell and lightning bolts flickered across the sky.

"Let's rest under these bushes a while, the storm can't last very long" said Felix. But nó sooner did they crouch there than something right behind them said, "Peasant brats, you didn't like us, didn't know how to treat us, now you sit here without any toys!"

Felix wheeled around, and recoiled, horrified. For the little huntsman and harpist rose from where he had thrown them, and stared at him with their dead eyes, groping for him with their hands. The little harpist touched the harp strings, making a weird *quinkalink*. The huntsman aimed his gun at Felix. "Just you wait," screeched the toys. "Wait, you boy and girl, we're Master Ink's obedient helpers! Master Ink will soon be here, and we'll have our revenge!"

The children were so aghast, they didn't care how hard the rain poured down or how loud the thunder crashed, or how the storm roared through the hemlocks, they ran away with all their might.

But when they got to the pond at the edge of the woods, Christlieb's doll rose out of the reeds where Felix had thrown her, and she croaked at them, "Little peasant brats, didn't like me, didn't know how to treat me, now you don't have

any toys! Just wait, you boy and girl, I'm Master Ink's obedient helper, he'll soon be here and we'll have our revenge!"
And she splashed and kicked great spurts of water at them
from the pond.

They ran on, but soon sank exhausted to the ground. A
humming and buzzing came after them. "Master Ink is coming!" Felix screamed—then he and Christlieb fainted with
fright.

When they awoke, they found themselves on a soft tuft of moss. The storm was over, the sun shone bright and friendly again, and raindrops hung like diamonds from the twigs of bushes and trees.

To Felix and Christlieb's surprise, their clothes were all dry, and they weren't the least bit cold. "The child from far away must have protected us," said Felix. They held out their hands, and called, "Oh please come back! We long for you so much, we can't live without you!"

Then a bright beam shone through the bushes, and when it touched the flowers they lifted up their heads. But no matter how beseechingly the children called, that was all there was to be seen. Their playmate did not appear. Sadly the children went home.

Their parents had been worried, and were glad to see
them.

Felix told them everything that had happened to them in the woods.

"Oh, what wild fancies," cried Lady von Brakel. "If that's what you dream up out there, you'd better stop going to the woods, and stay in the house with us."

But they did go again, for when they begged her, she let them go.

But the child did not appear. And whenever Felix and Christlieb came near the bushes or the duck pond, the huntsman, the harpist and the doll made fun of them and called them names. They couldn't endure it. Soon they stopped going to the woods and stayed at home feeling forlorn.

"Dear wife," said Sir Thaddeus to Lady von Brakel one day, "for some time I have been feeling strangely ailing, almost as if Master Ink had done me some harm. Ever since I hit him with the fly swatter and chased him away, all my joints have seemed heavy, as if they were filled with lead."

Indeed, Sir Thaddeus grew wearier and paler every day. He didn't walk through the fields anymore, he didn't putter about the house, but sat for hours steeped in thought. Often now he asked his children to tell about the child from far away. And every time they did, he smiled, but tears stood in his eyes.

He knew how they longed for their dear woods but were afraid to go. So one fine morning he gathered all his strength and said, "Come, children, we'll go together. With me along to protect you, those evil toys won't dare call you names or make fun of you."

He took Felix and Christlieb by the hand, and they went.

The woods seemed more alive than ever with sunshine, flower scent and bird song. Father and children sat down in the soft grass, and Sir Thaddeus spoke:

"Dear Felix, dear Christlieb, I must tell you that I, too, knew the child from far away. When I was your age the child came to me also, and played with me in these woods. I can't remember just when it stopped. But I must have forgotten, for when you told me I didn't believe you—yet deep inside my heart I knew you were telling the truth. These last days, though, I've been remembering my childhood very vividly, and I remember the child. Now, I feel the same longing you do—it's tearing at my heart! Oh child, appear to us!"

"Yes, come to us," called Felix and Christlieb, stretching out their arms.

They felt the child hovering about them, very, very near. But no matter how often they called to it, it did not show itself.

Sir Thaddeus sighed. He said, "I feel this is the last time I sit beside these bushes, under these trees . . ."

"No, Father, no," cried Felix and Christlieb, "you'll come and sit here with us again, many times!"

But the very next day Sir Thaddeus lay sick in bed. And three days later he was dead.

Oh how the children and their mother mourned!

And the four peasants of Brakelheim carried their lord to his grave. Soon after, two men almost as ugly as Master Ink came and took over the whole little property, the house and everything in it, in Count Cyprianus von Brakel's name. Sir Thaddeus had owed it all and much more to his cousin, they said.

Now Lady von Brakel and the children were penniless. They had to leave the village of Brakelheim and go to a relative who lived nearby. They made small bundles of a few bits of clothing the two men let them keep. Then, weeping, they left their home.

As they walked through the woods, past the stream so stormily rushing today, Lady von Brakel's grief overcame her and she fainted.

Christlieb and Felix knelt beside her and cried, "Oh, we're poor, unhappy children! Will no one have pity on us?"

That moment the stream's rushing seemed to turn into music; the bushes whispered knowingly; and soon the woods were all aglow with a marvelous light—from which the child from far away came forth, in such blinding radiance that Felix and Christlieb had to close their eyes. They felt the child's soft touch on them, and heard the child's fair voice, "Dear playmates, don't cry! I haven't stopped loving you, I never will. And I'll never leave you. Even when you can't actually see me, I'll float about you and help you with all my might to be happy and joyful all your days. Only hold fast to me in your hearts, and neither the evil Pepser nor any other enemy can harm you. And love me faithfully, always!"

"We will," cried Felix and Christlieb, "with our hearts and with our souls!"

When they were able to open their eyes again, the child had disappeared—and so had their sorrow. Now Lady von Brakel recovered from her faint, stood up and said, "Children, I saw you in a dream, you stood in a pure golden light, and that made me so glad!"

Comforted and of good spirits, they went on.

Their relative received them kindly, and everything was as the child from far away had said. Felix and Christlieb succeeded with whatever they undertook. They lived happily and joyfully on with their mother, and in their dreams they kept on playing with the child who never ceased to bring them the fairest wonders from its home.